Playing In the Mud

DEBBIE A. WEBSTER

Illustrated by: Dwight Nacaytuna

ISBN: Softcover   978-1-5434-4147-5
        EBook   978-1-5434-4148-2

Print information available on the last page

Rev. date: 08/14/2017

To order additional copies of this book, contact:
Xlibris
1-888-795-4274
www.Xlibris.com
Orders@Xlibris.com

To Brittany and Blake Webster

One bright sunny day in the summer, the weather was warm and crisp. The wind blew through your hair as if you were on a ride at the amusement park. The weather man said that it was going to be a nice day. The sun was shining through the children's bedroom windows. Brittany turned over, saw the sun and felt the warm breeze across her small little face. She was happy because she loved warm weather. On the other hand, Blake jumped out of bed and ran down the stairs as if the house was on fire.

The children went outside to enjoy the nice weather. Brittany rode her bike with her friends, while Blake sat on the front porch. Blake didn't stay outside long because he didn't have a thing to do. "What are you doing in the house so soon?" mother asked. He went to his room to take a nap. He was thinking about how he could make mud on a dry day like today.

Blake ran outside with his pail to get something to make mud. He went to the park to get some sand in his pail, and ran home with a big smile on his face. He went to the bathroom to put water in the pail, but it didn't make mud it just made wet sand. He needed his pail again, but the wet sand was still in it. Blake put the sand in his shoes so his mother couldn't find it, and went back outside to get more things. He came back with grass, still no mud. He put the wet grass in his toy box. He tried it again with rocks, still no mud. He put the rocks under the bed.

He tried everything, but dirt. Blake got tired and took a nap.
Brittany came in the house crying, pointing at the door she left
open, "It's raining." "Where is your brother"? Mother asked.
"I don't know."
"Go see if he's in his room, please."
Brittany went to the Blake's room.

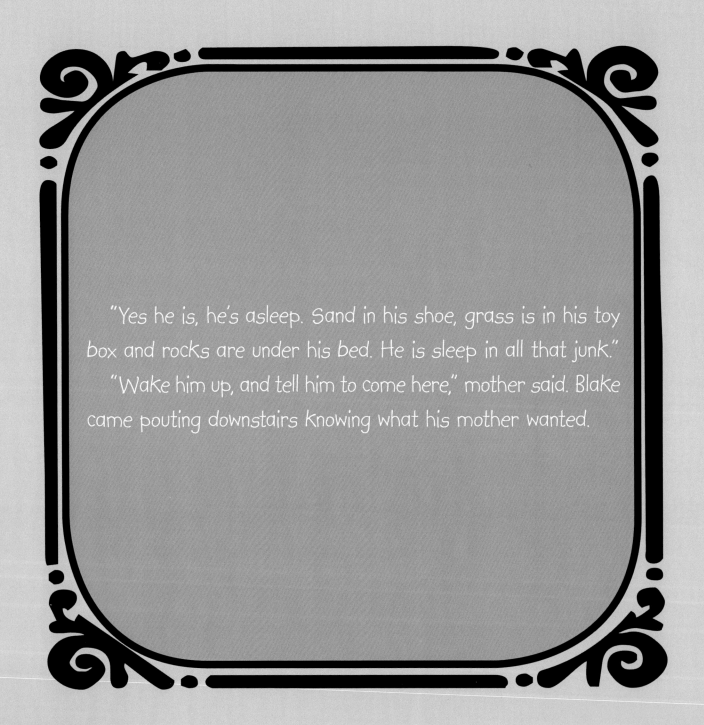

"Yes he is, he's asleep. Sand in his shoe, grass is in his toy box and rocks are under his bed. He is sleep in all that junk."

"Wake him up, and tell him to come here," mother said. Blake came pouting downstairs knowing what his mother wanted.

He just stood there with a *blank* look on his face thinking about what to say.

"Well, well, it didn't rain and I was trying to make mud."

"You can't make mud with the things you have in your room," mother said.

"I know that now."

"You need dirt" she said, "I have good news it's raining." Blake got the biggest smile on his face and ran to the window.

"Can I go outside please, please mommy can I?" "Wait until it stops."

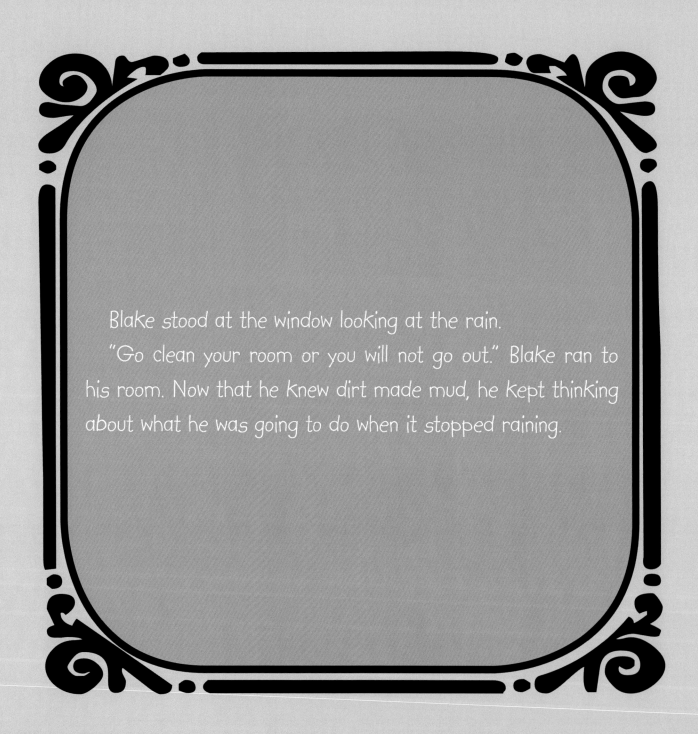

Blake stood at the window looking at the rain.

"Go clean your room or you will not go out." Blake ran to his room. Now that he knew dirt made mud, he kept thinking about what he was going to do when it stopped raining.

Blake cleaned his room and it was still raining. It was getting dark and the rain was still coming down in buckets. Blake was not looking to happy. Then he got to thinking, the more it rained the more mud he could play in. The next day came the rain had stopped. He ran outside to play in the mud. He was the happiest child on earth.

The End

Printed in the United States
By Bookmasters